PROMETHEUS ILLBOUND

PROMETHEUS ILLBOUND

ANDRÉ GIDE,
LILIAN ROTHERMERE

ISBN: 978-93-90015-92-4

Published: 1919

LECTOR HOUSE LLP
E-MAIL: lectorpublishing@gmail.com

PROMETHEUS ILLBOUND

BY

ANDRÉ GIDE

LITERAL TRANSLATION FROM THE FRENCH BY LILIAN ROTHERMERE

1919

PREFACE

The work of art is the exaggeration of an idea, says Gide in the epilogue of the "Prometheus Illbound." This is really the explanation of the whole book and of many other books of Gide.

His world is a world of abstract ideas, under the action of which most of his characters move as marionettes. "Time and space are the boards, which, with the help of our minds, have been set up by the innumerable truths of the universe as a stage for their own performances. And there we play our parts like determined, convinced, devoted and voluptuous marionettes."

That is the reason why there is a determinist atmosphere in his books and that even the disinterested act appears as the reaction of the mind on its own concept. Zeus, the banker, poses this disinterested act because his thought refuses or hesitates to admit it; the same thing happens with Lafcadio in the "Caves du Vatican" when he is on the point of murdering Amédée Fleurissoire.

The tyranny of ideas is the dominating force of his characters. Even his first writings—where one finds some of his best pages, which appear to be purely lyrical explosion—such as "Les Nourritures Terrestres" and "Le Voyage d'Urien," are really the songs of a mind which leads its life by the *concept* of eternal desire and detachment—a mind very near that of Nietzsche.

It is because of that tyranny of ideas that Gide is attracted by religious psychology. After all, Alissa of "La Porte Étroite" sacrifices her life and her happiness to her ideas. It is because of that also that one of the most daring books of the time, "L'Immoraliste," is written in the most moral way: the feelings are only described by their reaction on the brain. And this applies to nearly the whole work of Gide.

Even his concept of heroism is ruled by it. His heroes are monomaniacs of a thought which they believe or create ideal. His "Roi Candaule" is a man stupefied by the *idea* of his possessions.

That which does not nourish his brain is a reason for depression, and as love or passion absorbs the brain without nourishing it, he resents it. Every attempt of a purely amorous adventure is a failure, as well in "L'Immoraliste" as in the "Tentative Amoureuse."

On the contrary, when it becomes by struggle a problem for the brain it excites him. Alissa was really his only love, and he could not love Isabelle when she had lost her power of attraction through the revelation of the unknown she represented to his mind.

The exaltation of Gide is a Nietzschean exaltation—it is an exaltation caused by the power of mind.

The definition of genius he gives in "Prétextes" is very characteristic from that point of view. He calls it: "Le sentiment de la ressource."

His sensitiveness is the sensitiveness of the brain, which is so acute that it vibrates through his whole personality. From there comes the clear, logical form of his tales.

The book, "Prometheus Illbound," which we present to the English public to-day is one of the most characteristic books of Gide: a work of pure intellectual fantasy, where the subtle brain of the author has full play. It is the expression of the humorous side of a mind which must be ranked among the greatest of the world's literature.

LILIAN ROTHERMERE.

CONTENTS

PROMETHEUS ILLBOUND

PROMETHEUS ILLBOUND

Eagle, vulture or dove.

Victor Hugo.

In the month of May 189..., at two o'clock in the afternoon, this occurred which might appear strange:

On the boulevard leading from the Madeleine to the Opéra, a stout gentleman of middle age, with nothing remarkable about him but uncommon corpulence, was approached by a thin gentleman, who smilingly, thinking no harm, we believe, gave him back a handkerchief that he had just dropped. The corpulent gentleman thanked him briefly and was going his way when he suddenly leant towards the thin man and must have asked for information, which must have been given, for he produced from his pocket a portable inkpot and pens, which without more ado he handed to the thin gentleman, and also an envelope which up to this minute he had been holding in his hand. And those who passed could see the thin man writing an address upon it.—But here begins the strange part of the story, which no newspaper, however, reported: the thin gentleman, after having given back the pen and the envelope, had not even the time to smile adieu when the fat gentleman, in form of thanks, abruptly struck him on the face, then jumped in a cab and disappeared, before any of the spectators, stupefied with surprise (I was there), thought of stopping him.

I have been told since that it was Zeus, the banker.

The thin gentleman, visibly upset by the attentions of the crowd, insisted that he had hardly felt the blow, notwithstanding that the blood poured out of his nose and his cut-open lip. He begged them to be kind enough to leave him alone, and the crowd, on his insistence, slowly dispersed. Thus the reader will allow us to leave at present some one he will hear of sufficiently later on.

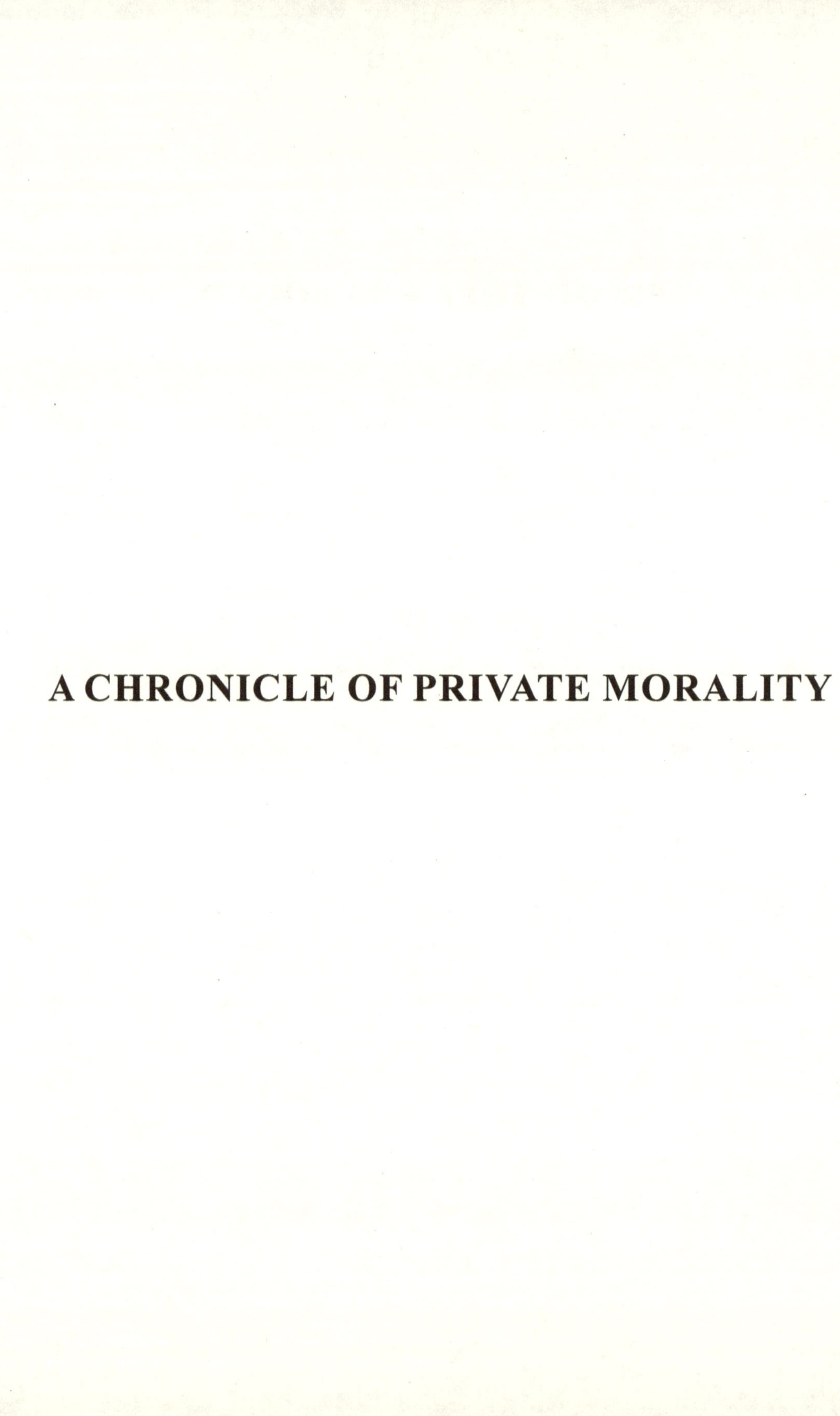

A CHRONICLE OF PRIVATE MORALITY

I

I WILL not speak of public morals, for there are none, but this reminds me of an anecdote:

When, on the heights of the Caucasus, Prometheus found that chains, clamps, strait-waistcoats, parapets, and other scruples, had on the whole a numbing effect on him, for a change he turned to the left, stretched his right arm and, between the fourth and fifth hours of an autumn afternoon, walked down the boulevard which leads from the Madeleine to the Opéra. Different Parisian celebrities passed continually before his eyes. Where are they going? Prometheus asked himself, and settling himself in a café with a book he asked: "Waiter, where are they going?"

THE HISTORY OF THE WAITER AND THE MIGLIONAIRE

—If his lordship could see them coming and going every day as I do, said the waiter, he would also ask where do they come from? It must be the same place, as they pass every day. I say to myself: Since they always return they cannot have found what they want. I now wait for his lordship to ask me: What are they looking for? and his lordship will see what I shall reply.

Then Prometheus asked: What are they looking for?

The waiter replied: Since they do not remain where they go, it cannot be happiness. His lordship may believe me or not, and, coming nearer, he said in a low voice: They are looking for their personalities;—His lordship does not live here?...

—No, said Prometheus.

—One can easily see that, said the waiter; Yes: personality; we call it here idiosyncrasy: Like me (for example), from what you see, you think I am just a waiter in a restaurant! Well! your lordship, no! It is by choice; you may believe me or not: I have an inner life: I observe. Personalities are the only interesting things; and then the relations between personalities. It is very well arranged in this restaurant; tables for three; I will explain the management later on. You will dine soon, will you not? We will introduce you....

Prometheus was a little tired. The waiter continued: Yes, tables for three, that is what I found the easiest: three gentlemen arrive; they are introduced; they are introduced (if they wish it, of course), for in my restaurant before dining you must give your name; then say what you do; so much the worse if you deceive each other. Then you sit down (not I); you talk (not I, of course)—but I put you in sympathy; I listen; I scrutinize; I direct the conversation. At the end of dinner I know three inner men, three personalities! They, no. I, you understand, I listen, I bring into relation; they submit to the relationship.... You will ask me: What do you gain by this? Oh, nothing at all! It pleases me to create relationships.... Oh! not for me!... It is what one could call an absolutely gratuitous act.

Prometheus appeared a little tired. The waiter continued: A gratuitous act! Does this convey nothing to you? — To me it seems extraordinary. I thought for a long time that this was the one thing that distinguished man from the animals — a gratuitous act. I called man an animal capable of a gratuitous act; — and then afterwards I thought the contrary; that man is the only being incapable of acting gratuitously; — gratuitously! just think; without reason — yes, I hear — shall we say without motive; incapable! then this idea began to fidget me. I said to myself: why does he do this? why does he do that? ... and yet I am not a determinist ... but that reminds me of an anecdote:

—I have a friend, my lord, you will hardly believe me, who he is a miglionaire. He is also intelligent. He said to himself: A gratuitous act? how to do it? And understand this does not only mean an act that brings no return.... No, but gratuitous: an act that has no motive. Do you understand? no interest, no passion, nothing. The act disinterested; born of itself; the act without aim, thus without master; the free act; the act Autochthon!

—Hey? said Prometheus.

—Listen well, said the waiter. My friend went out one morning, taking with him a bank-note of £20 in an envelope and a blow prepared in his hand.

The point was to find somebody without choosing him. So he drops his handkerchief in the street, and, to the man who picks it up (evidently kindly since he picked it up), the miglionaire:

—Pardon, sir, do you not know some one?

The other: — Yes, several.

The miglionaire: Then, sir, will you have the kindness to write his name on this envelope; here is a table, pens, and a pencil....

The other, good-naturedly, writes, then: — Now, sir, will you explain yourself...?

The miglionaire replies: It is on principle; then (I forgot to tell you he is very strong) he strikes him with the blow he had in his hand; then calls a cab and disappears.

Do you understand? — two gratuitous acts in one go! The bank-note of £20 sent to an address which he had not selected, and the blow given to a person who selected himself to pick up the handkerchief. No! but is it gratuitous enough? And the relation? I bet you have not seriously scrutinized the relationship; for, as the act is gratuitous, it is what we call here reversible: One receives £20 for a blow, and the other a blow for £20 ... then.... No one knows ... one is lost — think of it! A gratuitous act! There is nothing more demoralizing. — But my lord is beginning to be hungry; I beg his lordship's pardon; I forget myself, I talk too much.... Will his lordship kindly give me his name, — so that I can introduce him....

—Prometheus, said Prometheus simply.

—Prometheus! I was right, his lordship is a stranger here ... and his lordship's occupation is...?

—I do nothing, said Prometheus.

—Oh! no. No, said the waiter with an ingratiating smile.—Only to see his lordship, one knows at once that he is a man with an occupation.

—It is so long ago, stammered Prometheus.

—Never mind, never mind, continued the waiter. Anyway, his lordship need not be uneasy; in introducing I only say the name, if you like; but the occupation never. Come, tell me: his lordship's occupation is...?

—Making matches, murmured Prometheus, blushing.

There followed a painful silence, the waiter understanding that he should not have insisted, Prometheus feeling that he should not have answered.

In a consoling tone: Well! after all his lordship does not make them any more ... said the waiter. But then, what? I must write down something, I cannot write simply: Prometheus. His lordship has perhaps an avocation, a speciality.... After all, what can his lordship do?

—Nothing, again said Prometheus.

—Then let us say: Journalist.—Now, if his lordship will come into the restaurant; I cannot serve dinner outside. And he cried:—A table for three! one!...

By two doors two gentlemen entered; they could be seen giving their names to the waiter; but the introductions not having been asked for, without more ado the two men both sat down.

And when they had sat down:

II

—Gentlemen, said one of them,—if I have come to this restaurant, where the food is bad, it is only to talk. I have a horror of solitary meals, and this system of tables for three pleases me, as with two one might wrangle.... But you look taciturn?

—It is quite unintentional, said Prometheus.

—Shall I continue?

—Yes, please do.

—It seems to me quite possible that during lunch three people have time to become very well known to each other,—not losing too much time eating,—not talking too much; and avoiding trite topics; I mean to say mentioning only strictly individual experiences. I do not pretend that one is obliged to talk, but why come to this restaurant, where the food is bad, if conversation does not suit you?

Prometheus was very tired: the waiter leant over and whispered: That is Cocles. The one who is going to speak is Damocles.

Damocles said:

THE HISTORY OF DAMOCLES

Sir, if you had said that to me a month ago, I should have had nothing to say; but after what happened to me last month, all my ideas have changed. I will not speak of my old thoughts except to make you understand in what way I have changed.—Now, gentlemen, since thirty days I feel that I am an original, unique being, with a very singular destiny.—So, gentlemen, you can deduct that before I felt the contrary, I lived a perfectly ordinary life and made it my business to be as commonplace as possible. Now, however, I must admit that a commonplace man does not exist, and I affirm that it is a vain ambition to try to resemble everybody, for everybody is composed of each one, and each one does not resemble anybody. But never mind, I took the greatest pains to put things right; I drew up statistics; I calculated the happy medium—without understanding that extremes meet, that he who goes to bed very late comes across him who gets up very early, and that he who chooses the happy medium risks to fall between two stools.—Every night I went to bed at ten. I slept eight hours and a half. I was most careful in all my actions to copy the majority, and in all my thoughts the most approved opinions. Useless to insist.

But one day a personal adventure happened to me, the importance of which in the life of a well-ordered man as I was can only be understood later on. It is a precedent; it is terrible. And I received it.

III

Just imagine, one morning I received a letter. Gentlemen, I see by your lack of astonishment that I am telling my story very badly. I should have told you first that I did not expect any letters. I receive exactly two a year: one from my landlord to ask for the rent, and one from my bankers to inform me that I can pay it; but on the first of January I received a third letter.... I cannot tell you where from. The address was in an unknown hand. The complete lack of character shown in the writing, which was revealed to me by graphologists, whom I consulted, gave me no clue. The only indication the writing gave was one of great kindness; and here again certain of them inferred weakness. They could make nothing of it. The writing ... I speak, you understand, of the writing on the envelope; for in the envelope there was none; none—not a word, not a line. In the envelope there was nothing but a bank-note of £20.

I was just going to drink my chocolate; but I was so astonished that I let it get cold. I searched my mind ... nobody owes me money. I have a fixed revenue, gentlemen, and with little economies each year, notwithstanding the continual fall in the value of stock, I manage to live within my income. I expected nothing, as I have said. I have never asked for anything. My usual regular life prevents me from even wishing for anything. I gave much thought to the question after the best methods: *Cur, unde, quo, qua?*—From where, for where, by where, why? And this note was not an answer, for this was the first time in my life I questioned anything. I thought: it must be a mistake; perhaps I can repair it. This sum was intended no doubt for some one of the same name. So I looked in the Post Office Directory for a homonym, who was perhaps expecting the letter. But my name cannot be common, as in looking through that enormous book I was the only one of that name indicated.

I hoped to come to a better result by the writing on the envelope, and find out who sent the letter, if not to whom it was sent. It was then that I consulted the graphologists. But nothing—no nothing—they could tell me nothing; which only increased my distress. These £20 troubled me more and more every day; I would like to get rid of them, but I do not know what to do. For anyhow ... or if some one had given them to me, at least they deserve to be thanked. I should like to show my gratitude,—but to whom?

Always in the hope of something turning up, I carry the note with me. It does not leave me day or night. I am at its disposal. Before, I was banal but free. Now I belong to that note. This adventure has decided me; I was nothing, now I am somebody. Since this adventure I am restless; I search for people to talk to, and if

I come here for my meals it is because of this system of tables for three; among the people I meet here I hope one day to find the one who will know the writing on the envelope, here it is....

With these words Damocles drew from his breast a sigh and from his frock-coat a dirty yellow envelope. His full name was written there in a very ordinary handwriting.

Then a strange thing happened: Cocles, who up to that time had been silent, kept silent,—but suddenly raised his hand and made a violent effort to strike Damocles, the waiter catching his hand just in time. Cocles recovered himself and sadly made this speech, which can be only understood later on: After all, it is better so, for if I had succeeded in returning you the blow you would have believed it your duty to give me back the note and ... it does not belong to me.—Then, seeing that Damocles was waiting for a further explanation:—It was I, he added, pointing to the envelope, who wrote your address.

—But how did you know my name, cried Damocles, rather annoyed by the incident.

—By chance—quietly said Cocles;—in any case that is of little importance in this story. My story is even more curious than yours; let me tell you in a few words:

THE HISTORY OF COCLES

I have very few friends in the world; and before this happened I did not know of one. I do not know who was my father and I never knew my mother; for a long time I wondered why I lived.

I went out into the streets, searching for a determining influence from outside. I thought, the first thing that happens to me will decide my destiny; for I did not make myself as I am, too naturally kind for that. The first act, I knew, would give a motive to my life. Naturally kind, as I have said, my first act was to pick up a handkerchief. The one who dropped it had only gone three steps. Running after him I returned it to him. He took it without appearing surprised; no—the surprise was mine when he handed me an envelope—the same one that you see here.— Will you have the kindness, he said smilingly, to write here an address.—What address? I asked.—That, he replied, of any one you know.—So saying he placed near me all the materials to write with. Wishing to let myself go to exterior influence I submitted. But, as I told you, I have few friends in the world. I wrote the first name that came into my head at the moment, a name quite unknown to me. Having written the name I bowed—would have walked on—when I received a tremendous blow on my face.

In my astonishment I lost sight of my adversary. When I came to myself, I was surrounded by a crowd. All spoke at once. They would not let me alone. I could only rid myself of their attentions by assuring them that I was not hurt at all, even though my jaw caused me terrible pain and my nose was bleeding furiously.

The tumefaction of my face confined me to my room for a week. I passed my time thinking:

Why did he strike me?

It must have been a mistake. What could he have against me? I have never hurt anybody; nobody could wish me ill.—There must be a reason for ill-will.

And if it was not a mistake?—for the first time I was thinking. If that blow was intended for me! In any case, what does it matter! by mistake or not, I received it and ... shall I return it? I have told you, I am naturally good-hearted. And then there is another thing which worries me: the man who struck me was much stronger than I.

When my face was well and I could again go out, I looked everywhere for my adversary; yes, but it was to avoid him. Anyway, I never saw him again, and if I avoided him it was without knowing it.

But—and in saying this he leant towards Prometheus, you see to-day how everything joins up, it is becoming more complicated instead of less so: I understand that, thanks to my blow, this gentleman has received £20.

—Ah, but allow me! said Damocles.

—I am Cocles, sir, said he, bowing to Damocles;—Cocles! and I tell you my name, Damocles, for you must certainly be pleased to know to whom you owe your windfall....

—But....

—Yes—I know: we will not say to whom; we will say: from the suffering of whom.... For understand and do not forget that your gain came from my misfortune....

—But....

—Do not cavil, I beg you. Between your gain and my trouble there is a relation; I do not quite know which, but there is a relation....

—But, sir....

—Do not call me sir.

—But, my dear Cocles.

—Say simply Cocles.

—But once again, my best Cocles....

—No, sir,—no, Damocles,—and it is no use your talking, for I still wear the mark of the blow on my cheek ... it is a wound that I will show you at once.

The conversation becoming disagreeably personal, the waiter at this moment showed his tact.

IV

By a clever movement,—simply upsetting a full plate over Prometheus,—he suddenly diverted the attention of the other two. Prometheus could not restrain an exclamation, and his voice after the others seemed so profound that one realized that up to this minute he had not spoken.

The irritation of Damocles and Cocles joined forces.

—But you say nothing—they cried.

PROMETHEUS SPEAKS

—Oh, gentlemen, anything that I can say has so little importance.... I do not really see how ... and then the more I think.... No, truly I have nothing to say. You have each of you a history; I have none. Excuse me. Believe me it is with the greatest interest that I have heard you each relate an adventure which I wish ... I could.... But I cannot even express myself easily. No, truly you must excuse me, gentlemen. I have been in Paris less than two hours; nothing has as yet happened to me, except my delightful meeting with you, which gives me such a good idea of what a conversation can be between two Parisians, when they are both men of talent....

—But before you came here, said Cocles.

—You must have been somewhere, added Damocles.

—Yes, I admit it, said Prometheus.... But again, once more, it has absolutely no connexion....

—Never mind, said Cocles, we came here to talk. We have both of us, Damocles and I, already given our share; you alone bring nothing; you listen; it is not fair. It is time to speak Mr....?

The waiter, feeling instinctively that the moment had come for the introduction, quietly slipped in the name to complete the sentence:

—Prometheus—he said simply.

—Prometheus, repeated Damocles.—Excuse me, sir, but it seems to me that that name already....

—Oh! interrupted Prometheus quickly, that is not of the slightest importance.

—But if there is nothing of importance, impatiently cried the other two, why have you come here, dear Mr.... Mr....?

—Prometheus, replied Prometheus simply.

—Dear Mr. Prometheus—as I remarked a while ago, continued Cocles, this restaurant invites conversation, and nothing will convince me that your strange name is the only thing that distinguishes you; if you have done nothing, you are surely going to do something. What are you capable of doing? What is the most distinguishing thing about you? What have you that nobody else possesses? Why do you call yourself Prometheus?

Drowned beneath this flow of questions Prometheus bent his head and slowly and in a serious voice stammered...:

—What have I, gentlemen?—What have I?—Oh, I have an eagle.

—A what?

—Eagle—Vulture perhaps—opinions differ.

—An eagle! That's funny!—an eagle ... where is he?

—You insist on seeing it, said Prometheus.

—Yes, they cried, if it is not too indiscreet.

Then Prometheus, quite forgetting where he was, suddenly started up and gave a great cry, a call to his eagle. And this stupefying thing happened:

HISTORY OF THE EAGLE

A bird which from afar looked enormous, but which seen close to was not so very big after all, darkened for a moment the sky above the boulevard and sped like a whirlwind towards the café; bursting through the window, it put out Cocles' eye with one stroke of its wing and then, chirruping as it did so, tenderly indeed but imperiously, fell with a swoop upon Prometheus' right side.

And Prometheus forthwith undid his waistcoat and offered his liver to the bird.

V

There was a great disturbance. Voices now mingled confusedly, for some other people had come into the restaurant.

—But for goodness' sake, take care! cried Cocles.

His remark was unheard beneath the loud cries of:

—That! an eagle! I don't think!! Look at that poor gaunt bird! That ... an eagle!—Not much!! at the most, a conscience.

The fact is that the great eagle was pitiful to see—thin and mangy, and with drooping wings as it greedily devoured its miserable pittance, the poor bird seemed as if it had not eaten for three days.

Others, nevertheless, made a fuss and whispered insinuatingly to Prometheus: But, sir, I hope you do not think that this eagle distinguishes you in any way. An eagle, shall I tell you?—an eagle, we all have one.

—But ... said another.

—But we do not bring them to Paris, continued another.—In Paris it is not the fashion. Eagles are a nuisance. You see what it has already done. If it amuses you to let it eat your liver you are at liberty to do so; but I must tell you that it is a painful sight. When you do it you should hide yourself.

Prometheus, confused, murmured: Excuse me, gentlemen,—Oh! I am really sorry. What can I do?

—You ought to get rid of it before you come in, sir.

And some said: Smother it.

And others: Sell it. The newspaper offices are there for nothing else, sir.

And in the tumult which followed no one noticed Damocles, who suddenly asked the waiter for the bill.

The waiter gave him the following:

3 lunches (with conversation)	Fr. 30.00
Shop window	450.00
A glass eye for Cocles	3.50

... and keep the rest for yourself, said Damocles, handing the bank-note to the waiter. Then he quickly made off, beaming with joy.

The end of this chapter is much less interesting. Little by little the restaurant became empty. In vain Prometheus and Cocles insisted on paying their share of the bill—Damocles had already paid it. Prometheus said good-bye to the waiter and Cocles, and going back slowly to the Caucasus he thought: Sell it?—Smother it?... Tame it perhaps?...

THE IMPRISONMENT
OF PROMETHEUS

I

It was a few days after this that Prometheus, denounced by the over-zealous waiter, found himself in prison for making matches without a licence.

The prison was isolated from the rest of the world, and its only outlook was on to the sky. From the outside it had the appearance of a tower. In the inside Prometheus was consumed by boredom.

The waiter paid him a visit.

—Oh! said Prometheus smiling, I am so happy to see you! I was bored to death. Tell me, you who come from outside; the wall of this dungeon separates me from everything and I know nothing about other people. What is happening?— And you, first tell me what you are doing.

—Since your scandal, replied the waiter nothing much; hardly anybody has been to the restaurant. We have lost a great deal of time in repairing the window.

—I am greatly distressed, said Prometheus;—but Damocles? Have you seen Damocles? He left the restaurant so quickly the other day; I was not able to say good-bye. I am so sorry. He seemed a very quiet person, well-mannered, and full of scruples; I was touched when he told me so naturally of his trouble.—I hope when he left the table he was happier?

—That did not last, said the waiter. I saw him the next day more uneasy than ever. In talking to me he cried. His greatest anxiety was the health of Cocles.

—Is he unwell? asked Prometheus.

—Cocles?—Oh no, replied the waiter. I will say more: He sees better since he sees with only one eye. He shows every one his glass eye, and is delighted when he is condoled with. When you see him, tell him that his new eye looks well, and that he wears it gracefully; but add how he must have suffered....

—He suffers then?

—Yes, perhaps, when people do not sympathize with him.

—But then, if Cocles is well and does not suffer, why is Damocles anxious?

—Because of that which Cocles should have suffered.

—You advise me then strongly....

—To say it, yes, but Damocles thinks it, and that's what kills him.

—What else does he do?

—Nothing. This unique occupation wears him out. Between us, he is a man obsessed.—He says that without those £20 Cocles would not be miserable.

—And Cocles?

—He says the same.... But he has become rich.

—Really ... how?

—Oh! I do not know exactly;—but he has been talked about in the papers; and a subscription has been opened in his favour.

—And what does he do with it?

—He is an artful fellow. With the money collected he thinks of founding a hospital.

—A hospital?

—Yes, a small hospital for the one eyed. He has made himself director of it.

—Ah bah! cried Prometheus; you interest me enormously.

—I hoped you would be interested, said the waiter.

—And tell me ... the Miglionaire?

—Oh! he, he is a wonderful chap!—If you imagine that all that upsets him! He is like me: he observes.... If it would amuse you, I will introduce you to him—when you come out of this....

—Well, by the way, why am I here? Prometheus said at last. What am I accused of? Do you know, waiter, you seem to know everything?

—My goodness no, pretended the waiter. All that I know is that it is only preliminary detention. After they have condemned you, you will know.

—Well, so much the better! said Prometheus. I always prefer to know.

—Good-bye, said the waiter; it is late. With you it is astonishing how the time flies.... But tell me: your eagle? What has become of him?

—Bless me! I have thought no more of him, said Prometheus. But when the waiter had gone Prometheus began to think of his eagle.

HE MUST INCREASE BUT I MUST DECREASE

And as Prometheus was bored in the evening, he called his eagle.—The eagle came.

—I have waited a long time for thee, said Prometheus.

Why didst thou not call me before? replied the eagle.

For the first time Prometheus looked at his eagle, casually perched upon the twisted bars of the dungeon. In the golden light of the sunset he appeared more spiritless than ever; he was grey, ugly, stunted, surly, resigned, and miserable; he seemed too feeble to fly, seeing which Prometheus cried with pity.

—Faithful bird, he said to him, dost thou suffer?—tell me: what is the matter?

—I am hungry, said the eagle.

—Eat, said Prometheus, uncovering his liver.

The bird ate.

—I suffer, said Prometheus.

But the eagle said nothing more that day.

II

The next day at sunrise Prometheus longed for his eagle; he called it from the depth of the reddening dawn, and as the sun rose the eagle appeared. He had three more feathers and Prometheus sobbed with tenderness.

—How late thou comest, he said, caressing his feathers.

—It is because I cannot yet fly very fast, said the bird. I skim the ground....

—Why?

—I am so weak!

—What dost thou want to make thee fly faster?

—Thy liver.

—Very well, eat.

The next day the eagle had eight more feathers and a few days after he arrived before the dawn. Prometheus himself became very thin.

—Tell me of the world, he said to the eagle. What has happened to all the others?

—Oh! now I fly very high, replied the eagle; I see nothing but the sky and thee.

His wings had grown slowly bigger.

—Lovely bird, what hast thou to tell me this morning?

—I have carried my hunger through the air.

—Eagle, wilt thou never be less cruel?

—No! But I may become very beautiful.

Prometheus, enamoured of the future beauty of his eagle, gave him each day more to eat.

One evening the eagle did not leave him.

The next day it was the same.

He fascinated the prisoner by his gnawings; and, the prisoner, who fascinated him by his caresses, languished and pined away for love, all day caressing his feathers, sleeping at night beneath his wings, and feeding him as he desired.—The eagle did not stir night or day.

—Sweet eagle, who would have believed it?

—Believed what?

—That our love could be so charming.

—Ah! Prometheus....

—Tell me, my sweet bird! Why am I shut up here?

—What does that matter to thee? Am I not with thee?

—Yes; it matters little! but art thou pleased with me, beautiful eagle?

—Yes, if thou thinkest I am beautiful.

III

It was spring-time; around the bars of the tower the fragrant wisteria was in flower.

—One day we will go away, said the eagle.

—Really? cried Prometheus.

—Because I am now very strong and thou art thinner. I can carry thee.

—Eagle, my eagle!... Take me away.

And the eagle carried him away.

A CHAPTER WHILE WAITING THE NEXT ONE

That evening Cocles and Damocles met each other. They chatted together; but with a certain embarrassment.

—What can you expect? said Cocles, our points of view are so opposed.

—Do you think so? replied Damocles. My only desire is that we understand each other.

—You say that, but you only understand yourself.

—And you, you do not even listen to what I say.

—I know all that you would say.

—Say it then if you know it.

—You pretend to know it better than I do.

—Alas! Cocles, you get cross;—but for the love of God tell me what ought I to do?

—Ah! nothing more for me, I beg you; you have already given me a glass eye....

—Glass, in lack of a better, my Cocles.

—Yes—after having half blinded me.

—But it was not I, dear Cocles.

—It was more or less; and in any case you can pay for the eye—thanks to my blow.

—Cocles! forget the past!...

—No doubt it pleases you to forget.

—That's not what I mean to say to you.

—But what do you mean to say then? Go on, speak!

—You do not listen to me.

—Because I know all that you would say!...

The discussion, for want of something new began to take a dangerous turn, when both men were suddenly arrested by an advertisement which ran as follows:

THIS EVENING AT 8 O'CLOCK
IN THE
HALL OF THE NEW MOONS
PROMETHEUS DELIVERED
WILL SPEAK OF
HIS
EAGLE

At 8.30 the Eagle will be presented and will perform some tricks. At 9 o'clock a collection will be made by the waiter on behalf of Cocles' hospital.

—I must see that, said Cocles.

—I will go with you, said Damocles.

IV

In the Hall of the New Moons, at eight o'clock precisely, the crowd gathered.

Cocles sat on the left; Damocles on the right; and the rest of the public in the middle.

A thunder of applause greeted the entry of Prometheus; he mounted the steps of the platform, placed his eagle at the side of him, and pulled himself together.

In the hall there was a palpitating silence....

THE PETITIO PRINCIPII

—Gentlemen, began Prometheus, I do not pretend, alas! to interest you by what I am about to say, so I was careful to bring this eagle with me. After each tiresome part of my lecture he will play some tricks. I have also with me some indecent photographs and some fireworks, with which when I reach the most serious moments of my lecture I will try to distract the attention of the public. Thus, I dare to hope, gentlemen, for some attention. At each new head of my discourse I shall have the honour, gentlemen, to ask you to watch the eagle eating his dinner,—for, gentlemen, my discourse has three heads; I did not think it proper to reject this form, which is agreeable to my classical mind.—This being the exordium, I will tell you at once and without more ado, the first two heads of the discourse:

First head: One must have an eagle.

Second head: In any case, we all have one.

Fearing that you will accuse me of prejudice, gentlemen; fearing also to interfere with my liberty of thought, I have prepared my lecture only up to that point; the third head will naturally unfold from the other two. I will let inspiration have all its own way.—As conclusion, the eagle, gentlemen, will make the collection.

—Bravo! Bravo! cried Cocles.

Prometheus drank a little water. The eagle pirouetted three times round Prometheus and then bowed. Prometheus looked round the hall, smiled at Damocles and at Cocles, and as no sign of restlessness was as yet shown he kept the fireworks for later on, and continued:

V

—However clever a rhetorician I may be gentlemen, in the presence of such perspicacious minds as yours I cannot juggle away the inevitable *petitio principii* which awaits me at the beginning of this lecture.

Gentlemen, try as we may, we cannot escape the *petitio principii*. Now; what is a petition of principles? Gentlemen, I dare to say it: Every *petitio principii* is an affirmation of temperament; for where principles are missing, there the temperament is affirmed.

When I declare: You must have an eagle you may all exclaim: Why?—Now, what answer can I make in reply that will not bring us back to that formula, which is the affirmation of my temperament: I do not love men: I love that which devours them. Temperament, gentlemen, is that which must affirm itself. A fresh *petitio principii*, you will say. But I have demonstrated that every *petitio principii* is an affirmation of temperament; and as I say one must affirm one's temperament (for it is important), I repeat: I do not love men: I love that which devours them.—Now what devours man?—His eagle. Therefore, gentlemen, one must have an eagle. I think I have fully demonstrated this.

... Alas! I see, gentlemen, that I bore you; some of you are yawning. I could, it is true, here make a few jokes; but you would feel them out of place; I have an irredeemably serious mind.

I prefer to circulate among you some indecent photographs; they will keep those quiet who are feeling bored, which will enable me to go on.

Prometheus drank a drop of water. The eagle pirouetted three times round Prometheus and bowed. Prometheus went on:

CONTINUATION OF PROMETHEUS' LECTURE

—Gentlemen, I have not always known my eagle. That is what makes me deduce, by a process of reasoning which the logic books I never studied till a week ago, call by some particular name I have forgotten—that is what makes me deduce, I say, that, even though the only eagle here is mine, you all, gentlemen, have an eagle.

I have said nothing, up to the present, of my own history; firstly because, up to the present, I have not understood it. And if I decide to speak of it now it is because, thanks to my eagle, it now appears to me marvellous.

VI

—Gentlemen, as I have already said, my eagle was not always with me. Before his time I was unconscious and beautiful, happy and naked and unaware. Oh! Charming days! On the many-fountained sides of the Caucasus, lascivious Asia, naked too and unaware, held me in her arms.

Together we sported, tumbling in the valleys; the air sang, the water laughed, the simplest flowers were fragrant for our delight. And often we lay beneath spreading branches, among flowers which were the haunt of murmuring bees.

Asia wedded me, all laughter and then the murmuring swarms and the rustling leaves, with which was mingled the music of the streams, gently lulled us to the sweetest of slumbers. Around us all consented—all protected our inhuman solitude.—Suddenly one day Asia said to me: You should interest yourself in men.

I first had to find them.

I was willing enough to interest myself in them—but it was to pity them.

They lived in such darkness; I invented for them certain kinds of fire, and from that moment my eagle began. And it is since that day that I have become aware that I am naked.

At these words, applause arose from various parts of the hall. All of a sudden Prometheus broke into sobs.

The eagle flapped his wings and cooed.

With an agonizing gesture Prometheus opened his waistcoat and offered his tortured liver to the bird.

The applause redoubled.

Then the eagle pirouetted three times round Prometheus, who drank a few drops of water, and continued his lecture in these words:

VII

—Gentlemen, my modesty overcame me. Excuse me, it is the first time I speak in public. But now it is my sincerity which overcomes me. Gentlemen, I have been more interested in men than I have ever admitted. Gentlemen, I have done a great deal for men. Gentlemen, I have passionately, wildly, and deplorably loved men—and I have done so much for them—one can almost say that I have made them; for before, what were they? They existed, but had no consciousness of existence; I made this consciousness like a fire to enlighten them, gentlemen; I made it with all the love I bore them.—The first consciousness they had was that of their beauty. It is this which caused the propagation of the race. Men were prolonged in their posterity. The beauty of the first was repeated, equally, indifferently, uneventfully. It could have lasted a long time.—Then I grew anxious, for I carried in me already, without knowing it, my eagle's egg and I wanted more or better. This propagation, this piecemeal prolongation, seemed to me to indicate in them an expectancy—when in reality only my eagle was waiting. I did not know; that expectancy I thought was in man; that expectancy I put in man. Besides, having made man in my image, I now understood that in every man there was something hatching; in each one was the eagle's egg.... And then, I do not know; I cannot explain this.—All that I know is that, not satisfied with giving them consciousness of existence, I also wished to give them a reason for existence. So I gave them Fire, flame and all the arts which a flame nourishes. By warming their minds, I brought forth the devouring faith in progress. And I was strangely happy when their health was consumed in producing it. No more belief in good, but the morbid hope for better. The belief in progress, gentlemen, that was their eagle. Our eagle is our reason for existence, gentlemen.

Man's happiness grew less and less—but that was nothing to me: the eagle was born, gentlemen! I loved men no more, I loved what fed on them. I had had enough of a humanity without history.... The history of man is the history of their eagles, gentlemen.

VIII

Applause broke out here and there. Prometheus, abashed, excused himself:

—Gentlemen, I was lying: pardon me: it did not happen quite so quickly: No, I have not always loved eagles: For a long time I preferred men; their injured happiness was dear to me, because once having interfered I believed myself responsible, and in the evening every time I thought of it, my eagle, sad as remorse, came to eat.

He was at this time gaunt and grey, careworn and morose, and he was as ugly as a vulture.—Gentlemen, look at him now and understand why I tell you this; why I asked you to come here; why I entreat you to listen to me. It is because I have discovered this: the eagle can become very beautiful. Now, every one of us has an eagle; as I have just most earnestly asserted. An eagle?—Alas, a vulture perhaps! no, no, not a vulture, gentlemen!—Gentlemen, you must have an eagle....

And now I touch the most serious question:—Why an eagle?... Ah! Why?—let him say why. Here is mine, gentlemen; I bring him to you.... Eagle! Will you reply now? Anxiously Prometheus turned towards his eagle. The eagle was motionless and remained silent.... Prometheus continued in a distressed voice:

—Gentlemen, gentlemen, I have vainly questioned my eagle.... Eagle! speak now: every one listens to you.... Who sends you? Why have you chosen me? Where do you come from? Where do you go to? Speak: What is your nature? (The eagle remained silent.) No, nothing! Not a word! Not a cry!—I hoped he would speak to you at any rate; that is why I brought him with me.... Must I speak alone here?—All is silence!—All is silence!

What does it mean?... I have questioned in vain. Then turning towards the audience:

Oh! I hoped, gentlemen, that you would love my eagle, that your love would affirm his beauty.—That is why I gave myself up to him, that is why I filled him with the blood of my soul.... But I see I am alone in admiring him. Is it not enough for you that he is beautiful? Or do you not admit his beauty? Look at him at least. I have lived only for him—and now I bring him to you: There he is! As for me I live for him—but he ... but he, why does he live?

Eagle that I have nourished with the blood of my soul, whom with all my love I have caressed ... (here Prometheus was interrupted by sobs)—must I then leave the earth without knowing why I loved you, nor what you will do, nor what you will be, after me on the earth ... on the earth? I have ... asked in vain ... in vain....

The words choked in his throat—his voice could not be heard through his tears.—Pardon me, gentlemen,—he continued a little calmer; pardon me for saying such serious things, but if I knew more serious ones I would say them....

Perspiring, Prometheus wiped his face, drank some water, and added:

THE END OF PROMETHEUS' LECTURE

—I have only prepared my lecture up to this point....

... At these words there was a rustling among the audience; several, feeling bored, wished to go out.

—Gentlemen, cried Prometheus, I beseech you to stay, it will not be very long now; but the most important thing of all remains to be said, if I have not already persuaded you.... Gentlemen!—for goodness' sake.... Here! quickly: a few fireworks; I will keep the best for the end.... Gentlemen!—sit down again, I pray you; look: do not think I want to economize: I light six at a time.—But first, waiter, shut the doors.

The fireworks were more or less effective. Nearly every one sat down again.

—But where was I? cried Prometheus. I counted upon getting under weigh; disturbance has checked me.

—So much the better, cried some one.

—Ah! I know ... continued Prometheus. I wished to tell you again....

—Enough! enough!! cried voices from all parts of the hall.

... That you must love your eagle.

Several cried "Why?" ironically.

—I hear, gentlemen, some one asks me "Why?" I reply: Because then he will become beautiful.

—But if we become ugly?

—Gentlemen, I do not speak here words of self-interest....

—One can see that.

—They are words of self-devotion. Gentlemen, one must devote oneself to one's eagle.... (Agitation—many get up.) Gentlemen, do not move: I will be personal. It is not necessary to remind you of the history of Cocles and Damocles.—All here know it. Well—Well! I will tell them to their faces: the secret of their lives is in their self-devotion to their debt: You, Cocles, to your blow; you, Damocles, to your bank-note. Cocles, your duty was to make your scar deeper and your empty orbit emptier, oh! Cocles! yours, Damocles, to keep your bank-note, to continue owing it, owing it without shame, owing even more, owing it with joy. There is your eagle; there are other and more glorious ones. But I tell you this: the eagle will devour us anyway—vice or virtue—duty or passion,—cease to be commonplace and you cannot escape it. But....

(Here the voice of Prometheus was barely heard in the tumult)—but if you do not feed your eagle lovingly he will remain grey and miserable, invisible to all and sly; then you will call him conscience, not worthy of the torments he causes;

without beauty.—Gentlemen, you must love your eagle, love him to make him beautiful; for it is for his future beauty that you must love your eagle....

Now I have finished, gentlemen, my eagle will make the collection. Gentlemen, you must love my eagle.—In the meantime I will let off some fireworks....

Thanks to the pyrotechnic diversion, the assembly dispersed without too much trouble; but Damocles took cold on coming out of the hall.

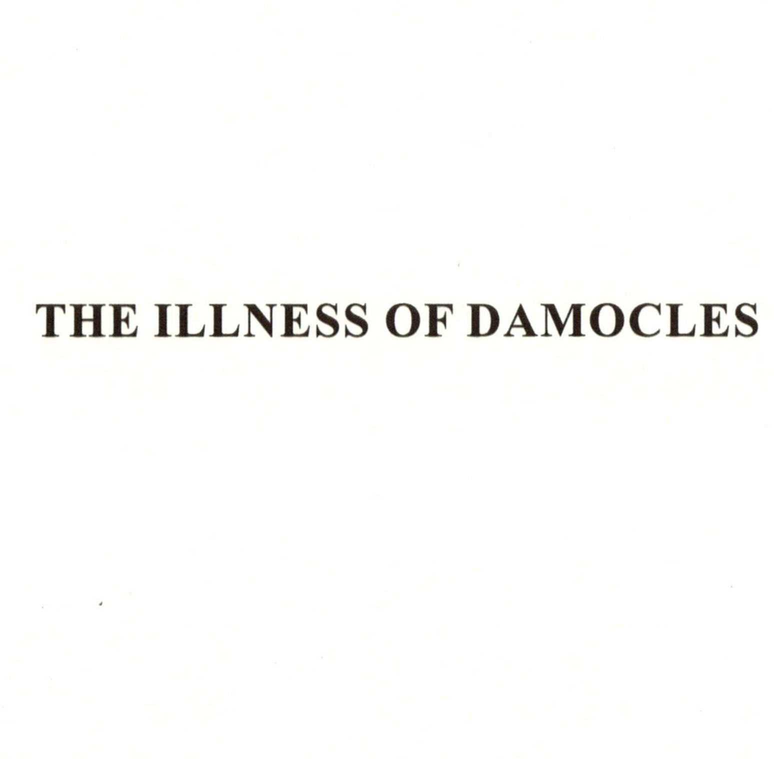

THE ILLNESS OF DAMOCLES

I

—You know that he is not at all well, said the waiter, seeing Prometheus a few days later.

—Who?

—Damocles—Oh! very bad:—it was coming out after your lecture that he was taken ill....

—But what is the matter?

—The doctors hesitate;—it is a very unusual illness ... a shrinkage of the spine....

—The spine?

—Yes, the spine.—At least, unless a miracle happens he must get worse. He is very low, I assure you, and you should go and see him.

—You go very often yourself?

—I? Yes, every day.—He is very anxious about Cocles; I bring him news every day.

—Why doesn't Cocles go to see him himself?

—Cocles?—He is too busy. Don't you remember your lecture? It has made an extraordinary effect upon him. He talks of nothing but self-devotion, and passes all his time looking in the streets for another blow, which may benefit some unknown Damocles. In vain he offers his other cheek.

—Why not tell the Miglionaire?

—I give him news every day. That is really the reason why I visit Damocles every day.

—Why does he not go and see Damocles himself?

—That is what I tell him, but he refuses. He does not wish to be known. And yet Damocles would certainly get well immediately if he knew his benefactor. I tell him all this, but he insists upon keeping his incognito—and I understand now that it is not Damocles but his illness which interests him.

—You spoke of introducing me?...

—Yes, at once, if you like.

They went off immediately.

II

Not knowing him ourselves, we have decided not to say very much about the waiter's friend, Zeus, but just to report these few remarks.

INTERVIEW OF THE MIGLIONAIRE

The waiter:—Is it not true that you are very rich?

The Miglionaire, half turning towards Prometheus:—I am richer than you can ever imagine. You belong to me; he belongs to me; everything belongs to me.—You think I am a banker; I am really something quite different. My effect on Paris is hidden, but it is none the less important. It is hidden because it is not continuous. Yes, I have above all the spirit of initiative. I launch; then, once the affair is set going, I leave it; I have nothing more to do with it.

The waiter:—Isn't it true that your actions are gratuitous?

The Miglionaire:—It is only I, only a person whose fortune is infinite, who can act with absolute disinterestedness; for man it is impossible. From that comes my love of gambling; I do not gamble for gain, you understand—I gamble for the pleasure of gambling. What could I gain that I do not possess already? Even time.... Do you know my age?

Prometheus and the waiter:—You appear still young, sir.

The Miglionaire:—Well, do not interrupt me, Prometheus.—Yes, I have a passion for gambling. My game is to lend to men. I lend, but it is not for pleasure. I lend, but it is sinking the capital. I lend, but with an air of giving.—I do not wish it known that I lend. I play, but I hide my game. I experiment; I play, as a Dutchman sows his seed; as he plants a secret bulb; that which I lend to men, that which I plant in man, I amuse myself by watching it grow; without that, man would be so empty!—Let me tell you my most recent experience. You will help me to analyse it. Just listen, you will understand later.

I went down into the street with the idea of making some one suffer for a gift I would make to another; to make one happy by the suffering of the other. A blow and a note of £20 was all that was necessary. To one the blow, and to the other the note. Is it clear? What is less clear is the way of giving them.

—I know it already, interrupted Prometheus.

—Oh, really, you know of it, said Zeus.

—I have met both Damocles and Cocles; it is precisely about them that I have come to speak to you:—Damocles looks and calls for you, he is very anxious; he is ill;—for goodness' sake go and see him.

—Sir, stop—said Zeus—I have no need of advice from anybody.

—What did I tell you? said the waiter.

Prometheus was going away, but suddenly turned again: Sir, pardon me. Excuse an indiscreet question. Oh! show it to me, I beg you! I should love so much to see it....

—What?

—Your eagle.

—But I have no eagle, sir.

—No eagle? He has no eagle! But....

—Not so much of one as I can hold in the hollow of my hand. Eagles (and he laughed), eagles! It is I who give them.

Prometheus was stupefied.

—Do you know what people say? the waiter asked the banker.

—What do they say?

—That you are God.

—I let them say so, said he.

III

Prometheus went to see Damocles; and then he went very often. He did not talk to him every time; but in any case the waiter gave him the news. One day he brought Cocles with him.

The waiter received them.

—Well, how is he? asked Prometheus.

—Bad. Very bad, replied the waiter. For three days the miserable man has not been able to take any food. His bank-note torments him; he looks for it everywhere; he thinks he may have eaten it;—he takes a purgative and thinks to find it in his stool. When his reason returns and he remembers his adventure, he is again in despair. He has a grudge against you, Cocles, because he thinks you have so complicated his debt that he no longer knows where he is. Most of the time he is delirious. At night there are three of us to watch him, but he keeps leaping upon his bed, which prevents us sleeping.

—Can we see him? said Cocles.

—Yes, but you will find him changed. He is devoured by anxiety. He has become thin, thin, thin. Will you recognize him?—And will he recognize you?

They entered on the tips of their toes.

THE LAST DAYS OF DAMOCLES

Damocles' bedroom smelt horribly of medicines. Low and very narrow, it was lighted gloomily by two night-lights. In an alcove, covered with innumerable blankets, one could see Damocles tossing about. He spoke all the time, although there was no one near him. His voice was hoarse and thick. Full of horror Prometheus and Cocles looked at each other; he did not hear them approach and continued his moaning as if he were alone.

—And from that day, he was saying, it seemed to me, both that my life began to have another meaning and that I could no longer live! That hated bank-note I believed I owed it to every one and I dared not give it to any one—without depriving all the others. I only dreamed of getting rid of it—but how?—The Savings Bank! but this increased my trouble; my debt was augmented by the interest on the money; and, on the other hand, the idea of letting it stagnate was intolerable to me; so I thought it best to circulate the sum; I carried it always upon me; regularly every week I changed the note into silver, and then the silver into another note. Nothing is lost or gained in this exchange. It is circular insanity.—And to this was added another torture: that it was through a blow given to another that I received this note!

One day, you know well, I met you in a restaurant....

—He is speaking of you, said the waiter.

—The eagle of Prometheus broke the window of the restaurant and put out Cocles' eye.... Saved!!—Gratuitously, fortuitously, providentially! I will slip my bank-note into the interstices of these events. No more debt! Saved! Ah! gentlemen! what an error.... It was from that day that I became a dying man. How can I explain this to you? Will you ever understand my anguish? I am still in debt for this note, and now it is no longer in my possession! I tried like a coward to get rid of my debt, but I have not acquitted it. In my nightmares I awake covered with perspiration. Kneeling down, I cry aloud: Lord! Lord! to whom do I owe this? I know nothing of it, but I owe—owing is like duty. Duty, gentlemen, is a horrible thing; look at me, I am dying of it.

And now I am more tormented than ever because I have passed this debt on to you, Cocles.... Cocles! it does not belong to you that eye, as the money it was bought with did not belong to me. And what hast thou that thou didst not receive? says the Bible ... received from whom? whom?? Whom??... My distress is intolerable.

The wretched man spoke in short, sharp jerks; his voice grew inarticulate, choked as it was by gasps, sobs and tears. Anxiously Prometheus and Cocles listened; they took each other's hand and trembled. Damocles said, seeming to see them:

Debt is a terrible duty, gentlemen ... but how much more terrible is the remorse of having wished to evade a duty.... As if the debt could cease to exist because it was transferred to another.... But your eye burns you, Cocles!—Cocles!! I am certain it burns you, your glass eye; tear it out!—If it does not burn you, it ought to burn you, for it is not yours—your eye ... and if it is not yours it must be your brother's ... whose is it? whose? Whose??

The miserable man wept; he became delirious and lost strength; now and again fixing his eyes on Prometheus and Cocles he seemed to recognize them, crying:

—But understand me for pity's sake! The pity I claim from you is not simply a compress on my forehead, a bowl of fresh water, a soothing drink; it is to understand me. Help me to understand myself, for pity's sake! *This* which has come to me from I know not where, to whom do I owe it? to whom?? to Whom??—And, in order to cease one day from owing it one day, believing, I made with *this* a present to others! To others!!—to Cocles—the gift of an eye!! but it is not yours, that eye, Cocles! Cocles!! give it back. Give it back, but to whom? to whom? to Whom??

Not wishing to hear more, Cocles and Prometheus went away.

IV

—There, you see, said Cocles, coming down the stairs, the fate of a man who has grown rich by another's suffering.

—But is it true that you suffer? asked Prometheus.

—From my eye occasionally, said Cocles, but from the blow, no more; I prefer to have received it. It does not burn any more; it has revealed to me my goodness. I am flattered by it; I am pleased about it. I never cease to think that my pain was useful to my neighbour and that it brought him £20.

—But the neighbour is dying of it, Cocles, said Prometheus.

—Did you not tell him that one must nourish one's eagle? What do you expect? Damocles and I never could understand each other, our points of view are entirely opposed.

Prometheus said good-bye to Cocles and ran to the house of Zeus, the banker.

—For goodness' sake, show yourself! he said, or at least make yourself known. The miserable man is dying. I could understand your killing him since that is your pleasure; but let him know at least who it is that is killing him—that he may be at peace.

The Miglionaire replied:—I do not wish to lose my prestige.

V

The end of Damocles was admirable; he pronounced a little while before his last hour some words which drew tears from the most unbelieving and made pious people say: How edifying! The most notable sentiment was the one expressed so well in these words: I hope at any rate that he will not have felt the loss of it.

—Who? asked some one.

—He, said Damocles, dying; he who gave me ... something.

—No! it was Providence, cleverly replied the waiter.

Damocles died after hearing these comforting words.

THE FUNERAL

—Oh! said Prometheus to Cocles, leaving the chamber of death,—all that is horrible! The death of Damocles upsets me. Is it true that my lecture can have been the cause of his illness?

—I cannot say, said the waiter, but I know that at any rate he was greatly moved by all that you said of your eagle.

—Of our eagle, replied Cocles.

—I was so convinced, said Prometheus.

—That is why you convinced him.... Your words were very strong.

—I thought that no one paid any attention and I insisted.... If I had known that he would listen so attentively....

—What would you have said?

—The same thing, stammered Prometheus.

—Then?

—But I would not say the same thing now.

—Are you no longer convinced?

—Damocles was too much so.... I have other ideas about my eagle.

—By the way, where is he?

—Do not fear, Cocles. I have my eye on him.

—Good-bye. I shall wear mourning, said Cocles. When shall we see each other again?

—But ... at the funeral, I suppose. I will make a speech there. I ought to repair in some way the damage I have done. And afterwards I invite you to the funeral feast in the restaurant exactly where we saw Damocles for the first time.

VI

At the funeral there were not many people; Damocles was very little known; his death passed unnoticed except for those few interested in his history. Prometheus, the waiter, and Cocles found themselves at the cemetery, also a few idle listeners of the lecture. Every one looked at Prometheus, as they knew he was to speak; and they said: "What will he say?" for they remembered what he had said before. Before Prometheus began to speak great astonishment was caused by the fact that he was unrecognizable; he was fat, fresh, smiling; smiling so much that his conduct was judged a little indecent, as smiling still he advanced to the edge of the grave, turned his back on it, and spoke these simple words:

THE HISTORY OF TITYRUS

—Gentlemen who are kind enough to listen to me, the words of Scripture which serve as text for my brief discourse to-day are these:

Let the dead bury their dead. We will therefore occupy ourselves no more with Damocles.—The last time that I saw you all together was to hear me speak of my eagle; Damocles died of it; leave the dead ... it is nevertheless because of him, or rather thanks to his death, that now I have killed my eagle....

—Killed his eagle!!! cried every one.

—That reminds me of an anecdote.... Let us grant I have said nothing.

I

In the beginning was Tityrus.

And Tityrus being alone and completely surrounded by swamps was bored.—Then Menalcas passed by, who put an idea into the head of Tityrus, a seed in the swamp before him. And this idea was the seed and this seed was the Idea. And with the help of God the seed germinated and became a little plant, and Tityrus in the evening and in the morning knelt before it, thanking God for having given it to him. And the plant became tall and great, and as it had powerful roots it very soon completely dried up the soil around it, and thus Tityrus had at last firm earth on which to set his feet, rest his head, and strengthen the works of his hands.

When this plant had grown to the height of Tityrus, Tityrus tasted the joy of sleeping stretched under its shadow. Now, this tree, being an oak-tree, grew enormously; so much so that soon Tityrus' hands were no longer sufficient to till and hoe the earth around the oak—to water the oak, to prune, to trim, to decorticate, to destroy the caterpillars, and to ensure in due season the picking of its many and diverse fruits. He engaged, therefore, a tiller and a hoer, and a trimmer and a decorticator, and a man to destroy the caterpillars, and a man to water the oak, and two or three fruit boys. And as each had to keep strictly to his own speciality, there was a chance of each person's work being well done.

In order to arrange for the paying of the wages, Tityrus had to have an accountant, who soon shared with a cashier the worries of Tityrus' fortune; this grew like the oak.

Certain arguments arising between the trimmer, and the pruner, and the depilator — as to where each man's work began and finished, Tityrus saw the necessity of an arbitrator, who called for two lawyers to expose both sides of the question.

Tityrus took a secretary to record their judgments, and as they were only recorded for future reference, there had to be a keeper of the rolls.

On the soil meanwhile houses appeared one by one, and it was necessary to have police for the streets, to guard against excesses. Tityrus, overcome by work, began to feel ill. He sent for a doctor who told him to take a wife — and finding the work too much for him, Tityrus was forced to choose a sheriff, and he himself was therefore appointed mayor. From this time he had only very few hours of leisure, when he could fish with a line from the windows of his house, which still continued to open on the swamp.

Then Tityrus instituted bank holidays so that his people might enjoy themselves; but as this was expensive and no one was very rich, Tityrus, in order to be able to lend them all money, first began by raising it from each of them separately.

Now the oak in the middle of the plain (for in spite of the town, in spite of the effort of so many men, it had never ceased to be the plain), the oak, as I said, in the middle of the plain, had no difficulty in being placed so that one of its sides was in shadow and the other in the sunshine. Under the oak then, on the shady side Tityrus rendered justice; on the sunny side he fulfilled his natural necessities. And Tityrus was happy, for he felt his life was useful to others and fully occupied.

II

Man's effort can be intensified. Tityrus' activity seemed to grow with encouragement; his natural ingenuity caused him to think of other means of employment. He set to work to furnish and decorate his house. The suitable character of the hangings and the convenience of each object were much admired. Industrious, he excelled in empiricism; he even made a little hook to hang his sponges on the wall, which after four days he found perfectly useless. Then Tityrus built another room by the side of his room, where he could arrange the affairs of the nation; the two rooms had the same entrance, to indicate that their interests were the same; but because of the one entrance which supplied both rooms with air, the two chimneys would not draw at the same time, so that when it was cold and a fire was lighted in one, the other was full of smoke. The days therefore that he wished for a fire, Tityrus was forced to open his window.

As Tityrus protected everything and worked for the propagation of the species, a time came when the slugs crawled on his garden paths in such abundance that he did not know where to step for fear of crushing them and finally resigned.

He invited a woman with a circulating library to come to the town, with whom he opened a subscription. And as she was called Angèle he became accustomed to go there every three days and pass his evenings with her. And by this means Tityrus learnt metaphysics, algebra, and theodicy. Tityrus and Angèle began to practise together successfully various accomplishments, and Angèle showing particular taste for music, they hired a grand piano upon which Angèle played the little tunes which between times he composed for her.

Tityrus said to Angèle: So many occupations will kill me. I am at the end of my tether; I feel that I am getting used up, these consolidated interests intensify my scruples, and as my scruples grow greater I grow less. What is to be done?

—Shall we go away? said Angèle to him.

—I cannot go: I have my oak.

—Suppose you were to leave it, said Angèle.

—Leave my oak! You don't mean it!

—Is it not large enough now to grow alone?

—But I am attached to it.

—Become unattached, replied Angèle.

And a little while after, having realized strongly that after all, occupations, responsibilities, and other scruples could hold him no more than the oak, Tityrus smiled and went off, taking with him the cash-box and Angèle, and towards the end of the day walked with her down the boulevard which leads from the Madeleine to the Opéra.

III

That evening the boulevard had a strange look. One felt that something unusually grave was going to happen. An enormous crowd, serious and anxious, overflowed the pavement, spreading on to the road, which the Paris police, placed at intervals, with great trouble kept free. Before the restaurants, the terraces disproportionately enlarged by the placing of chairs and tables, made the obstruction more complete and rendered circulation impossible. Now and again an onlooker impatiently stood upon his chair for an instant—the time that one could beg him to get down. Evidently all were waiting; one felt without doubt that between the two pavements upon the protected route something was going to pass. Having found a table with great difficulty and paid a large price for it, Angèle and Tityrus installed themselves in front of two glasses of beer and asked the waiter:

—What are they all waiting for?

—Where does your lordship come from? said the waiter. Does not your lordship know that every one is waiting to see Melibœus? He will pass by between 5 and 6 ... and there—listen: I believe one can already hear his flute.

From the depths of the boulevard the frail notes of a pipe were heard. The crowd thrilled with still greater attention. The sound increased, came nearer, grew louder and louder.

—Oh, how it moves me! said Angèle.

The setting sun soon threw its rays from one end of the boulevard to the other. And, as if issuing from the splendour of the setting sun, Melibœus was at last seen advancing—preceded by the simple sound of his flute.

At first nothing could be clearly distinguished but his figure, but when he drew nearer:

—Oh, how charming he is! said Angèle. In the meantime Melibœus as he arrived opposite Tityrus, ceased to play his flute, stopped suddenly, saw Angèle, and every one realized that he was naked.

Oh! said Angèle, leaning upon Tityrus, how beautiful he is! what strong thighs he has! His playing is adorable!

Tityrus felt a little uncomfortable.

—Ask him where he is going, said Angèle.

—Where are you going? questioned Tityrus.

Melibœus replied:—Eo Romam.

—What does he say? asked Angèle.

Tityrus:—You would not understand, my dear.

—But you can explain it to me, said Angèle.

—Romam, insisted Melibœus.... Urbem quam dicunt Romam.

Angèle:—Oh, it sounds delicious! What does it mean?

Tityrus:—But my dear Angèle, I assure you it is not so delightful as it sounds; it means quite simply that he is going to Rome.

—Rome! said Angèle dreamily. Oh, I should love so much to see Rome!

Melibœus, resuming his flute, once more began to play his primæval melody, and at the sound, Angèle, in a passion of excitement, raised herself, stood up, drew near; and as Melibœus' arm was bent to her hand, she took it, and thus the two together went on their way along the boulevard; further, further they went, gradually vanished from sight, and disappeared into the finality of the twilit dusk.

The crowd, now unbridled in its agitation, became more and more tumultuous. On all sides one heard the questions: What did he say?—What did he do?—Who was that woman?—And when, a few minutes later, the evening papers appeared, a furious curiosity swept over them like a cyclone, and it was suddenly divulged that the woman was Angèle, and that this Melibœus was a naked person who was going to Italy.

Then, all their curiosity having died down, the crowd streamed off like water flowing away and the main boulevards were deserted.

And Tityrus found himself alone, completely surrounded by the swamp.

Let us grant that I have said nothing.

An irrepressible laughter shook the audience for several seconds.

—Gentlemen, I am happy that my story has amused you, said Prometheus, laughing also. Since the death of Damocles I have found the secret of laughter. For the present I have finished, gentlemen. Let the dead bury the dead and let us go quickly to lunch.

He took the waiter by one arm and Cocles by the other; they all left the cemetery; after passing the gates, the rest of the assembly dispersed.

—Pardon me, said Cocles. Your story was charming, and you made us laugh.... But I do not quite understand the connexion....

—If there had been more you would not have laughed so much, said Prometheus. Do not look for too much meaning in all this. I wanted above all to distract you, and I am happy to have done so; surely I owed you that? I wearied you so the other day.

They found themselves on the boulevards.

—Where are we going? said the waiter.

—To your restaurant, if you do not mind, in memory of our first meeting.

—You are passing it, said the waiter.

—I do not recognize it.

—It is all new now.

—Oh, I forgot!... I forgot that my eagle.... Don't trouble: he will never do it again.

—Is it true, said Cocles, what you say?

—What?

—That you have killed him?

—And that we are going to eat him?... Do you doubt it? said Prometheus. Have you looked at me?—When he was alive, did I dare to laugh?—Was I not horribly thin?

—Certainly.

—He fed on me long enough. I think now that it is my turn.

—A table! Sit down! Sit down, gentlemen!

—Waiter, do not serve us: as a last remembrance, take the place of Damocles.

The meal was more joyful than it is possible to say. The eagle was found to be delicious, and at dessert they all drank his health.

—Has he then been useless? asked one.

—Do not say that, Cocles!—his flesh has nourished us.—When I questioned him he answered nothing, but I eat him without bearing him a grudge: if he had made me suffer less, he would have been less fat; less fat, he would have been less delectable.

—Of his past beauty, what is there left.

—I have kept all his feathers.

It is with one of them that I write this little book. May you, rare friend, not find it too foolish.

EPILOGUE

TO ENDEAVOUR TO MAKE THE READER BELIEVE
THAT IF THIS BOOK IS SUCH AS IT IS, IT IS NOT
THE FAULT OF THE AUTHOR

One does not write the books one wants to.

Journal des Goncourt.

The history of Leda made such a great stir and covered Tyndarus with so much glory that Minos was not much disturbed to hear Pasiphaë say to him: "It can't be helped. I do not like men."

But later: "It is very provoking (and it has not been easy!) I trusted that a God had hidden there. If Zeus had done his share I should have produced a Dioscurus; thanks to this animal, I have only given birth to a calf."

Lector House believes that a society develops through a two-fold approach of continuous learning and adaptation, which is derived from the study of classic literary works spread across the historic timeline of literature records. Therefore, we aim at reviving, repairing and redeveloping all those inaccessible or damaged but historically as well as culturally important literature across subjects so that the future generations may have an opportunity to study and learn from past works to embark upon a journey of creating a better future.

This book is a result of an effort made by Lector House towards making a contribution to the preservation and repair of original ancient works which might hold historical significance to the approach of continuous learning across subjects.

HAPPY READING & LEARNING!

LECTOR HOUSE LLP
E-MAIL: lectorpublishing@gmail.com